JERRY SPINELLI

My Fourth of July

Illustrated by
LARRY DAY

NEAL PORTER BOOKS
HOLIDAY HOUSE / NEW YORK

To the Grand- and Great-Grandkids
All 36 of you
(and counting) —J. S.

To safety and happiness for all —L.D.

Neal Porter Books

Text copyright © 2019 by Jerry Spinelli
Illustrations copyright © 2019 by Larry Day
All Rights Reserved
HOLIDAY HOUSE is registered in the U.S. Patent and Trademark Office.
Printed and bound in October 2018 at Toppan Leefung, DongGuan City, China.
The artwork was created with pencil, pen, and ink with watercolor and gouache on watercolor paper.
www.holidayhouse.com
First Edition
1 3 5 7 9 10 8 6 4 2

Library of Congress Cataloging-in-Publication Data
Names: Spinelli, Jerry, author. | Day, Larry, 1956- illustrator.
Title: My Fourth of July / Jerry Spinelli ; Illustrated by Larry Day.
Description: First edition. | New York : Holiday House, [2019] | "Neal Porter
Books." | Summary: A young boy and his family celebrate his favorite day,
Independence Day, by seeing a parade, having a picnic, watching a talent
show, and enjoying fireworks.
Identifiers: LCCN 2018028291 | ISBN 9780823442881 (hardcover)
Subjects: | CYAC: Fourth of July—Fiction. | Family life—Fiction. |
Community life—Fiction.
Classification: LCC PZ7.S75663 My 2019 | DDC [E]—dc23 LC record available
at https://lccn.loc.gov/2018028291

Noise!
I wake up.
I rush to the front window.
Parade! Drums! Cymbals!
Pinwheels! Flags! Tricycles!
It's the best day of all—
the Fourth of July!

I join the parade.
Grown-ups laugh and wave.
And point—I'm still in my pajamas!

When I get back, Dad is fetching the wagon. Hooray! He's home all day. Mama is in the kitchen, getting the picnic ready.

The pie is in the oven.
"What kind?" I ask her.
"You'll see," she says.
She always says, "You'll see."
The pie is always cherry crumb.

"Time to do my job?" I ask.
Mama hands me a shaker. "Get to work," she says.
I get to add the final touch—
a sprinkle of paprika on the deviled eggs.
Everything goes into the wagon.
Hot dogs.
Hot dog rolls.
Mustard.
Chopped onions.
Relish.
Pickles.

I look at the clock. I call to everybody: "Hurry!"
(I'm in charge of hurrying.)
There are only twenty-five picnic tables at the park.
We must not be late.

The wagon is filling up. Peanut butter–filled celery boats. Potato salad. Napkins. Tablecloth. Red, white, and blue cupcakes.

In goes the surprise in a white box.
There's always a surprise.
"What is it?" I ask. (I always ask.)

"You'll see." (Mama always says.)

Paper cups, plastic forks . . .
are we ready?

"Wait!" I shout. "Don't forget
the pie!"
(I'm in charge of not forgetting.)
Finally . . . out the door!

Mama hands me a banana. I'm so excited I forgot to eat breakfast.

Down the street to the railroad tracks . . .
Look! Black cloud . . . thunder . . .
Oh no—storm coming!

Yahoo! It's a train rumbling 'round the bend.
Flags flutter from the flanks of the great engine.
We wave at the engineer.

Down the path by the creek to the park.
"Hurry! Hurry!"
I grab the pickle jar and run ahead.
I plunk it on an empty table.
It's ours!

I can't wait. I beg for the surprise.
Mama sighs. "Oh, okay—go ahead."

I tear open the white box. . . .
Chocolate-covered strawberries! Big as plums.
Mom and Dad watch me. They can't stand it.
They gobble their surprises too.

For this one best day, the park is my backyard.

Face painting! I'm a raccoon.

Three-legged sack race! My friend Henry and I come in last.
We're laughing too hard to care.

Back to the table. Food! Eat!
We cook our hot dogs on the grill in the gazebo.
We wait our turn. I like mine with black stripes.

Talent show at the bandshell!
There's my neighbor Sally. She sings a song called
"Somewhere Over the Rainbow." I'm bogglepussed. Sally—
my next-door neighbor Sally—sings like an angel!

Concert!
At the gazebo The Tootletown Ten plays zippy
music. Little kids rush the stage of the gazebo to
dance. Parents too. Here come Mom and Dad!

Back at the bandshell, the biggest
flag I've ever seen is unrolling
behind the stage. We stand for "The
Star-Spangled Banner." The whole
park is silent and still.

Back to the picnic table. Eat! Eat!

Noseball race!
I win!

Run to the zoo!

Quack at
the ducks . . .

The goat makes
me laugh . . .

Monkey fingers
reaching . . .

More food! I'm becoming
a potato–pickle–hot dog–cupcake pie.
"Slow down," Mama says. But she doesn't
mean it. She's smiling.
The shadows are getting long. The sun is in the trees.
The best part of the best day is coming . . .
fireworks!
I eat the last deviled egg.
We toss the trash, give
away the pickles.

All that's left for the wagon
is the tablecloth.
"Hurry!" I say.
(I'm in charge of getting a good place.)

We find one, on the outfield
slopes of the baseball field.
Soon we're surrounded.
I think everybody in town is here.
"Five thousand people!" Dad says.

Shadows creep across the field . . .

all the way to me . . .

Oh, the minutes crawl

as I slide back in my wagon.

It's the longest wait

there ever is.

A *thump* in the dark . . . sudden
umbrella of lights . . . five thousand
faces aglow . . .

Fireworks!

Pinwheels and gushers . . .

comets and twisters . . .

My eyes cannot hold the wonders I see.
My heart is cheering.

A cannon-booming volley . . .

I hold my ears . . .

I scream with joy . . .

And it's over.

Car lights flashing. Smoke drifting from the baseball field.
It smells like burnt toast.

And once again I feel something I haven't felt since the
third of July. I feel sleepy.

The tablecloth becomes a pillow.
Into the wagon I go. My own little
train, with Dad as engineer.

Through the park . . .
across the creek . . .
down the path . . .

I see nothing but stars. There are only the stars and my wagon and me. I am overfilled in every way. I have seen too much . . . run too long . . . been too happy.
I close my eyes.

I am in charge of sleeping.